P9-DMZ-397

For Miss Emma, the original Dogosaurus Rex
—A. S.

To Cleo, the best dog in the world
—K. H.

Henry Holt and Company • *Publishers since 1866*
175 Fifth Avenue, New York, New York 10010 • mackids.com

Henry Holt® is a registered trademark of Macmillan Publishing Group, LLC.
Text copyright © 2017 by Anna Staniszewski
Illustrations copyright © 2017 by Kevin Hawkes
All rights reserved.

Library of Congress Cataloging-in-Publication Data is available.
ISBN 978-0-8050-9706-1

Our books may be purchased in bulk for promotional, educational, or business use.
Please contact your local bookseller or the Macmillan Corporate and Premium Sales Department at
(800) 221-7945 ext. 5442 or by e-mail at MacmillanSpecialMarkets@macmillan.com.

First Edition—2017 / Designed by Patrick Collins
The art for this book was created using sepia-toned pencil, as well as watercolor and acrylic washes on Bristol vellum.
Printed in China by Toppan Leefung Printing Ltd., Dongguan City, Guangdong Province

1 3 5 7 9 10 8 6 4 2

DogoSAURUS Rex

Anna Staniszewski

illustrated by
Kevin Hawkes

HENRY HOLT AND COMPANY
NEW YORK

3 3133 02882 0579

Central Rappahannock Regional Library
1201 Caroline Street
Fredericksburg, VA 22401

Ben couldn't wait to find the best dog in the world.
At the shelter, there were cute dogs and funny dogs
and loud dogs and smelly dogs.

None of them were quite right.

Then Ben saw a large cage in the corner.
"She's perfect!" he said. "I'll call her Sadie."
"ROAR!" said Sadie, wagging her tail.
"That dog sure has a strange bark,"
said Ben's mom.

Ben couldn't wait to show off his new pet. He used a garden hose for a leash and walked Sadie around town.

"She's kind of funny looking," said the neighborhood kids. "Does she know any tricks?"

"Sit, Sadie!" Ben called.
Sadie sat . . . on top of a car.

"Roll over, Sadie!" Ben called.
Sadie rolled over . . . right through a fruit stand.

"Fetch, Sadie!" Ben called.
Sadie ran off and came back . . .
with a mail truck.

"I think it's best if you take your
pet home," said a police officer.

But when Ben brought Sadie home, she couldn't fit through the front door.

"You'll have to build her a doghouse," said Ben's mom.

So Ben started building and building until . . .

...he'd built the biggest doghouse in town!
Sadie seemed to like her new home.
"You're the best dog in the world,"
Ben said, rubbing her belly.
Sadie closed her eyes.
"Roar," she said.

The next morning, Ben took Sadie out to do her business. She did lots of it. Lots and lots of it.

"Clean up after your pet!" a neighbor cried.

Ben plugged his nose, grabbed a shovel, and got to work.

Then it was time to give Sadie a bath. Ben gathered up all the soap in the house and took her to the lake. Sadie jumped into the water ... and drank it all in one gulp.

"Don't come back!"
the lifeguard yelled.

When they got home, Sadie's belly rumbled for dinner.
Ben poured out some dog food. Sadie ate the whole bag
. . . and all the rest of the food in the house.

"This dog sure is a lot of trouble," said Ben's mom. "We might have to bring her back to the shelter."

Ben hugged Sadie tight. He had to find a way to keep her.

The next day, Ben walked Sadie through
town. Everyone avoided her.

Then a shout rang out from the fruit
stand: "Stop! Thief!"

Ben knew just what to do.

"Sit, Sadie!" he called.
Sadie sat right in the robber's path . . .

but the thief jumped into a mail truck
and got away.

"Roll over, Sadie!" Ben called.
Sadie rolled over in front of the
robber's truck...

but the thief ran into the farmer's field
and got away.

"Fetch, Sadie!" Ben called.
Sadie barreled after the robber.
Ben had never seen her run so fast.

And when she came back, she had the thief clenched
in her teeth!
Everyone in town cheered.

"That's quite a pet you have there," said the police officer. "I think I might have a job for her."

"So do I," said the mailman.

"So do I," said the farmer.

Soon, Sadie was the most popular dog in town.
And Ben knew he'd be able to keep her forever.

"You're the best dog in the world," said Ben,
rubbing Sadie's belly.

Sadie closed her eyes. "Roar," she said.